Rooted in His Strength

POSTPARTUM PROMISES

A 30-DAY DEVOTIONAL FOR NEW MOMS

Written by

MICHELLE BEETZ

The Lord gives
his people strength.
The Lord blesses
them with peace.

—Psalm 29:11 NLT

Dear Mama,

Postpartum is more than a phase—it's a
sacred unfolding. You're not just healing a
body. You're becoming something new.

Each page of this devotional is written for
the moments no one sees: the 3 a.m. feedings,
the quiet cries, the waves of joy and
guilt, the "Who am I now?" questions.

This book won't give you all the answers—but it
will remind you of what's always been true:
God is here. His grace is enough.
And you are still wholly loved in your becoming.

Let each day breathe life into your weary places.
Let these promises root you deeper in His strength.

With love,
Michelle

I know the Lord
is always with me.
I will not be shaken,
for he is right beside me.

—Psalm 16:8

Table of Contents

He Sees You While You Heal

🔲 Scripture:

"The Lord is close to the brokenhearted; He rescues those whose spirits are crushed." – Psalm 34:18 (NLT)

You may feel invisible in this season — behind the diapers, the tears, the unwashed hair. But God sees you. Not just as a mother, but as His daughter. As you heal — physically, emotionally, spiritually — He is near. He isn't waiting for you to bounce back. He's sitting beside you, holding space for your exhaustion and your becoming. There is no shame in slowness. No guilt in tears. Only grace.

🔲 Breath Prayer:

"Jesus, You see me. Be near to me while I heal."

🔲 Rooted Reflection:

Where do you need God's closeness most right now?

____

____

____

____

Your Body Did a Holy Thing

Scripture:

"I praise you because I am fearfully and wonderfully made." – Psalm 139:14 (NLT)

Your body is not broken. It's a miracle. Even if it feels unfamiliar or wounded, it deserves awe. You carried life. You made space. And now, you're still giving — through feeding, comforting, showing up. God is not ashamed of your softness or scars. He calls it sacred. Honor your body by offering it compassion. It is still holy.

Breath Prayer:

"God, thank You for this body You made and carried life through."

Rooted Reflection:

What would it look like to see your body through God's eyes?

You Were Chosen for This Baby

Scripture:

"Before I formed you in the womb, I knew you." – Jeremiah 1:5 (NLT)

This baby isn't an accident. And neither is your motherhood. God doesn't make mistakes. Even in your uncertainty, He is sure. Even when you question if you're doing enough, He whispers: "I picked you." You were chosen — not for perfection, but for presence. For the kind of love that only you can give.

Breath Prayer:

"Lord, remind me I was chosen for this sacred role."

Rooted Reflection:

What doubts can you lay down and replace with truth?

____

____

____

____

____

– DAY 4 –

Sleep-Deprived but Still Loved

Scripture:

"Come to me, all of you who are weary and carry heavy burdens, and I will give you rest." – Matthew 11:28 (NLT)

God sees the 2 a.m. feedings. The cries you can't soothe. The nights that never seem to end. And He's not disappointed. He's not waiting for you to wake up cheerful or parent perfectly. He's offering rest — not just for your body, but for your soul. When you collapse into bed, know that you're already held in His arms.

Breath Prayer:

"Jesus, be my rest when sleep can't reach me."

Rooted Reflection:

What burden can you lay down in exchange for His rest?

____

____

____

____

____

It's Okay to Miss Who You Were

Scripture:

"There is a time for everything... a time to grieve and a time to dance." – Ecclesiastes 3:1, 4 (NLT)

You love your baby fiercely — but you may also miss the woman you were before. That's okay. Grief and gratitude can live in the same breath. You are not less, you are more. Becoming a mother means letting go of old things and embracing new growth. But you're still in there — evolving, not erasing.

Breath Prayer:

"God, help me hold both the joy and the grief gently."

Rooted Reflection:

What part of yourself do you want to nurture again?

____

____

____

____

____

Scripture:

"Pour out your heart to Him, for God is our refuge." – Psalm 62:8 (NLT)

Joy. Guilt. Gratitude. Overwhelm. It can all exist at once. You don't have to pretend. God can hold your full range of emotions. He created them — not to shame you, but to help you process and heal. So cry when you need to. Laugh when you can. Be honest. There is no emotion too messy for Him.

Breath Prayer:

"God, I give You my whole heart — every feeling included."

Rooted Reflection:

What emotions are you trying to hide that God is already holding?

____

____

____

____

Small Moments Are Still Sacred

Scripture:

"Do not despise these small beginnings." – Zechariah 4:10 (NLT)

Changing diapers. Rocking a baby at 3 a.m. Warming bottles. These things may feel repetitive — invisible even. But in God's eyes, they are sacred. Love isn't always loud. It's in the quiet sacrifice, the steady showing up. Heaven honors what the world overlooks. Don't underestimate the holiness in the mundane.

Breath Prayer:

"Lord, remind me that my smallest offerings matter to You."

Rooted Reflection:

What "small" moment today can you honor as holy?

____

____

____

____

____

Scripture:

"And I am certain that God... will continue His work until it is finally finished." – Philippians 1:6 (NLT)

It's easy to feel like you're getting it wrong. But motherhood isn't a test — it's a transformation. You're not supposed to have it all figured out. You are growing just as your baby is growing. There is grace for your learning curve. God isn't grading you — He's guiding you.

Breath Prayer:

"Jesus, be gentle with me while I grow."

Rooted Reflection:

Where are you holding yourself to impossible standards?

____

____

____

____

You Don't Have to Do It Alone

Scripture:

"Share each other's burdens." – Galatians 6:2 (NLT)

There's a lie that says a "good mom" does it all. But God never asked you to do this alone. You were created for community, not isolation. Asking for help doesn't make you weak — it makes you wise. Let people in. Let God send support in unexpected ways. You weren't meant to carry this all yourself.

Breath Prayer:

"Lord, help me receive support without guilt."

Rooted Reflection:

Who or what is God placing in your life to support you right now?

____

____

____

____

____

The Bond Is Still Building

Scripture:

"We love each other because He loved us first." – 1 John 4:19 (NLT)

Not every mother feels an instant bond. And that doesn't make you a bad mom — it makes you human. Sometimes connection grows slowly, day by day, through feeding, eye contact, rocking, or whispered prayers. God is growing that love in you. Give it time. There is no shame in needing space to connect. Love will come. It already is.

Breath Prayer:

"Jesus, help me trust the bond You're growing between us."

Rooted Reflection:

What is one way you've shown love, even if it didn't feel "magical"?

____

____

____

____

– DAY 11 –

You Are Still You

Scripture:

"I knew you before I formed you in your mother's womb." – Jeremiah 1:5 (NLT)

Becoming a mother doesn't erase your identity — it expands it. The woman you were before motherhood still matters. She's still in there, growing, learning, becoming more. God doesn't ask you to give up who you are. He invites you to bring your whole self into this new role — gifts, quirks, dreams and all.

Breath Prayer:

"God, help me remember that I am still Your beloved daughter."

Rooted Reflection:

What parts of yourself do you miss and want to reconnect with?

____

____

____

____

____

– DAY 12 –
God Isn't Measuring You

Scripture:

"The Lord doesn't see things the way you see them." – 1 Samuel 16:7 (NLT)

You may feel like you're falling short — not doing enough, not being enough. But God's standard isn't perfection. It's presence. He's not tallying feedings or comparing you to other moms. He sees your heart. He delights in your effort. He measures in grace, not guilt.

Breath Prayer:

"Jesus, help me let go of comparison and live in grace."

Rooted Reflection:

What "not enough" lies do you need to replace with truth today?

____

____

____

____

____

– DAY 13 –
Healing Isn't Linear

Scripture:

"He heals the brokenhearted and bandages their wounds." – Psalm 147:3 (NLT)

Some days feel strong. Some don't. Healing — emotionally, physically, spiritually — doesn't follow a straight line. And that's okay. God isn't impatient with your process. He's walking beside you, tenderly tending every ache. There is no deadline for your healing. You are safe in His pace.

Breath Prayer:

"Lord, be gentle with me as I heal."

Rooted Reflection:

What part of your healing journey needs more compassion and less pressure?

____

____

____

____

– DAY 14 –
You're Not Behind

Scripture:

"For everything there is a season, a time for every activity under heaven." – Ecclesiastes 3:1 (NLT)

It's tempting to look around and feel like you're behind. Behind on recovery. Behind on housework. Behind on "getting your life back." But you're not late — you're in process. God's timeline is never rushed. This season may feel slow, but slow is not wrong. It's sacred. You are right where you need to be.

Breath Prayer:

"God, help me trust Your timing over mine."

Rooted Reflection:

Where have you been pressuring yourself to "catch up"?

____

____

____

____

____

– DAY 15 –
Grace Covers the Gaps

Scripture:

"My grace is all you need. My power works best in weakness." – 2 Corinthians 12:9 (NLT)

You won't always get it right. You'll have moments of frustration, forgetfulness, or doubt. But God's grace covers what you can't. You don't have to do this perfectly — just faithfully. When you feel like you've come to the end of yourself, He fills in the rest. That's not failure. That's divine partnership.

Breath Prayer:

"Lord, fill in the places where I feel empty."

Rooted Reflection:

What guilt or pressure can you surrender to grace today?

It's Okay to Ask for Help

Scripture:

"Two people are better off than one... If one person falls, the other can reach out and help." – Ecclesiastes 4:9–10 (NLT)

You don't have to be everything to everyone. You were never meant to carry motherhood alone. God designed us for community, for support, for shared strength. Asking for help doesn't make you weak — it makes you wise. Let others step in, not because you can't, but because you don't have to do it all.

Breath Prayer:

"God, help me ask for what I need without shame."

Rooted Reflection:

Who can you invite into your circle of support this week?

Your Love is Enough

Scripture:

"Perfect love expels all fear." – 1 John 4:18 (NLT)

You may question if you're doing enough — giving enough, being enough. But love isn't measured in milestones or routines. It's in the soft glances, the tired snuggles, the whispered prayers. Your love — even when weary — is enough. God's love through you is covering every gap and growing something eternal.

Breath Prayer:

"Lord, let me rest in the truth that love is enough."

Rooted Reflection:

Where are you trying to "prove" instead of simply love?

____

____

____

____

____

The Comparison Trap Isn't Worth It

Scripture:

"Pay careful attention to your own work… for we are each responsible for our own conduct." – Galatians 6:4–5 (NLT)

Scrolling social media. Hearing how someone else's baby sleeps through the night. It's easy to fall into the trap of comparison — but it steals your joy and peace. God didn't design you to parent like everyone else. He designed you for your child. That is sacred. And that is more than enough.

Breath Prayer:

"God, guard my heart from comparison and help me celebrate my own story."

Rooted Reflection:

What would it look like to fully embrace your unique journey today?

____

____

____

– DAY 19 –
It's Okay to Feel Lonely

Scripture:

"Even if my father and mother abandon me, the Lord will hold me close." – Psalm 27:10 (NLT)

Postpartum can be one of the loneliest seasons — even when surrounded by people. But God is not distant. He draws close to the isolated and brokenhearted. Your quiet tears are heard. Your ache is noticed. You are not alone, even when it feels like it. Let Him hold you through the stillness.

Breath Prayer:

"Jesus, be my companion in the lonely moments."

Rooted Reflection:

Where do you need to feel God's closeness today?

____

____

____

____

____

You're Building Something Beautiful

Scripture:

"Unless the Lord builds a house, the work of the builders is wasted."
– Psalm 127:1 (NLT)

This season can feel like a blur of repetition — feedings, naps, tears, more feedings. But every small act of love is building something eternal. You're laying down a foundation of safety, presence, and love that your child will carry forever. God sees the long view — and what you're building matters deeply.

Breath Prayer:

"Lord, help me see the beauty in what feels ordinary."

Rooted Reflection:

What small action today could be part of something bigger than you realize?

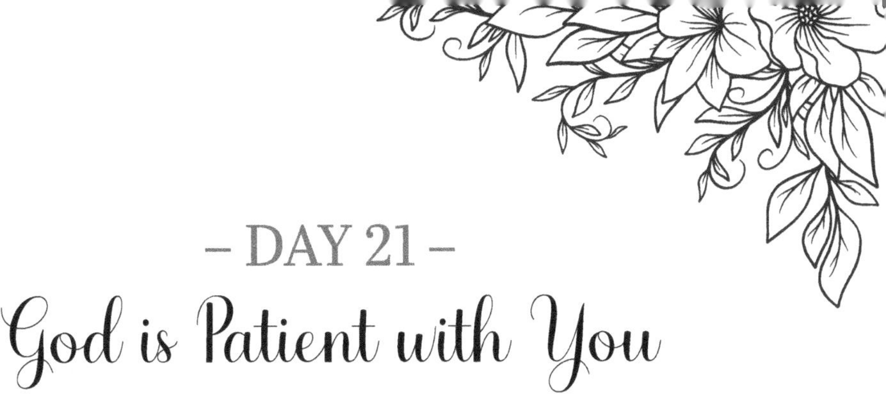

God is Patient with You

Scripture:

"The Lord is compassionate and merciful, slow to get angry and filled with unfailing love." – Psalm 103:8 (NLT)

You may lose patience with your baby. With yourself. With this whole season. But God never loses patience with you. He understands your frustration. He holds your exhaustion. He doesn't expect you to get it all right — just to come back to Him. There is room to fall apart and still be fully loved.

Breath Prayer:

"God, be patient with me — and help me be patient with myself."

Rooted Reflection:

Where have you been harsh on yourself that God has already offered grace?

____

____

____

____

Even Jesus Rested

Scripture:

"Then Jesus said, 'Let's go off by ourselves to a quiet place and rest awhile.'" – Mark 6:31 (NLT)

If the Son of God needed rest, you do too. This is not weakness — it's wisdom. Rest isn't lazy or indulgent. It's how your soul breathes. Let go of the guilt. Let the dishes wait. Your worth is not tied to your productivity. Rest is holy. And God invites you into it.

Breath Prayer:

"Lord, lead me to stillness. Help me rest without guilt."

Rooted Reflection:

What would it look like to honor rest as a spiritual practice this week?

____

____

____

____

____

Joy Will Find You Again

Scripture:

"Weeping may last through the night, but joy comes with the morning." – Psalm 30:5 (NLT)

If postpartum has felt like a cloud, like a season of tears and fog — know this: joy is not gone forever. It's waiting for you. Sometimes it shows up in unexpected giggles, warm sunshine, or your baby's sleepy smile. It may come slowly, but it will return. God has joy for you — still.

Breath Prayer:

"God, hold my heart and make space for joy again."

Rooted Reflection:

What small joy can you thank God for today — even if it feels fragile?

____

____

____

____

____

Scripture:

"Be strong and courageous... For the Lord your God is with you wherever you go." – Joshua 1:9 (NLT)

No matter how isolated this season may feel, you are not walking it by yourself. God is with you in the nursery, in the night feeds, in the silence and the chaos. And you are also part of a sisterhood of mothers — seen and unseen — who understand. You are surrounded. You are supported.

Breath Prayer:

"Jesus, remind me I'm never truly alone."

Rooted Reflection:

Where in your day can you invite God to walk with you more closely?

____

____

____

____

____

Your Child is a Gift – and So Are You

🟦 Scripture:

"Whatever is good and perfect is a gift coming down to us from God our Father." – James 1:17 (NLT)

It's easy to focus on your child as a miracle — and they are. But you, too, are a gift. To them. To your family. To this world. You are not "just a mom." You are a daughter of God, chosen and equipped for this season. Your life carries purpose. Your heart carries beauty. Don't forget your worth.

🟦 Breath Prayer:

"God, help me see myself as a gift, not just a giver."

🟦 Rooted Reflection:

What would change if you truly believed that you were a gift, too?

____

____

____

____

– DAY 26 –
You're Doing Holy Work

Scripture:

"So whether you eat or drink, or whatever you do, do it all for the glory of God." – 1 Corinthians 10:31 (NLT)

It may not feel holy to wash bottles, wipe tears, or clean up spit-up. But every act of care is sacred when done with love. Motherhood is full of quiet, unseen moments — and God is in all of them. He doesn't just dwell in churches. He's in nurseries, kitchens, and middle-of-the-night rocking chairs. You are serving Him when you serve your child.

Breath Prayer:

"Lord, remind me this small work matters to You."

Rooted Reflection:

What part of your routine can you start viewing as sacred?

____

____

____

____

He's Strengthening You One Day at a Time

Scripture:

"Your strength will equal your days." – Deuteronomy 33:25 (NLT)

You don't need strength for tomorrow yet. Just today. God gives us what we need moment by moment — not all at once, but always right on time. You don't have to figure out next week or next year. Just breathe, trust, and take the next faithful step. You're not walking alone.

Breath Prayer:

"Jesus, give me strength for this one day."

Rooted Reflection:

Where have you been trying to carry more than just today?

____

____

____

____

Your Weakness is Welcome Here

Scripture:

"My grace is all you need. My power works best in weakness." – 2 Corinthians 12:9 (NLT)

God doesn't flinch at your limits. He moves toward them. When you feel undone, overwhelmed, unsure — that's not the end of the story. It's the beginning of grace. You don't need to pretend you're strong when you're not. Your weakness makes room for His strength to shine.

Breath Prayer:

"God, I give You my weakness — meet me there."

Rooted Reflection:

Where do you need to be gentler with yourself today?

____

____

____

____

____

Your Story Is Still Being Written

Scripture:

"And I am certain that God... will continue His work until it is finally finished." – Philippians 1:6 (NLT)

This season is just one chapter, not the whole book. There is more ahead. More joy. More purpose. More healing. You're not stuck — you're being shaped. God is not finished writing your story. He's holding the pen, and His plans for you are full of goodness.

Breath Prayer:

"Lord, keep writing my story with grace."

Rooted Reflection:

What is God teaching you in this chapter that could shape the next?

____

____

____

____

You Are Rooted in His Love

Scripture:

"Then Christ will make His home in your hearts as you trust in Him. Your roots will grow down into God's love and keep you strong." – Ephesians 3:17 (NLT)

You may feel shaky at times, but underneath it all — you are rooted. Not in how much you accomplish. Not in how perfect you parent. You are rooted in His love. That love doesn't change when you cry, fall short, or feel lost. It is your steady place. And from it, you will keep growing — strong, beautiful, and unshakable.

Breath Prayer:

"God, root me deeper in Your love today."

Rooted Reflection:

What would change if you mothered from a place of being deeply loved?

____

____

____

____

Thank you for allowing this devotional to be part of your postpartum journey.

I pray that each page has reminded you of your strength, your worth, and the nearness of God in every season.

You are not alone, Mama. You are rooted in His strength and growing in grace each day.

With heartfelt gratitude,

Michelle Beetz

www.ingramcontent.com/pod-product-compliance
Lightning Source LLC
Chambersburg PA
CBHW040845010826

48978CB00012BB/902